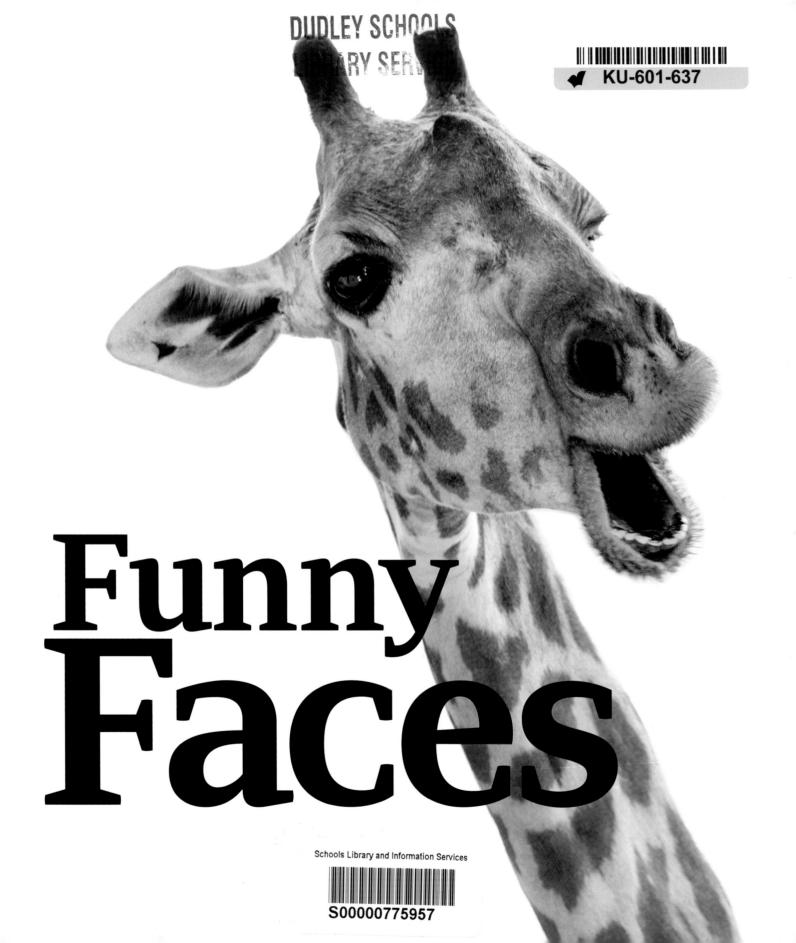

Funny
Faces

First published in 2014
by **black dog books**,
an imprint of Walker Books Australia Pty Ltd
Locked Bag 22, Newtown
NSW 2042 Australia
www.walkerbooks.com.au

The moral rights of the author have been asserted.

National Library of Australia Cataloguing-in-Publication entry:
Norman, Mark Douglas, author.
Funny faces / Mark Norman.
ISBN: 978 1 922179 96 8 (paperback)
For primary school age.
Subjects: Animals – Juvenile literature.
590

Typeset in Adobe Garamond Pro and Adamant BG

Printed and bound in China

Image credits: front cover, p10, p30 (tarsier) © **haveseen/Shutterstock.com**; back cover (hoopoe) © **IbajaUsap/Shutterstock.com**; p1 (giraffe) © **prapass/Shutterstock.com**; p2 (owl), p5 (eagle), p25 (cockatoo), p28, p31 (insect) © **Eric Isselee/Shutterstock.com**; p3 (fish) © **bluehand/Shutterstock.com**; p4 (walrus) © **Elena Yakusheva/Shutterstock.com**; p5 (cricket) © **Tsekhmister/Shutterstock.com**, (gecko) © **Michiel de Wit/Shutterstock.com**; p6 (elephant seal) © **Eduardo Rivero/Shutterstock.com**; p7 (elephant) © **tristan tan/Shutterstock.com**; p8, p30 (trident bat) © **Ivan Kuzmin/Shutterstock.com**; p9 (dolphin) © **treasure dragon/Shutterstock.com**; p11 (dragonfly) © **Peter Schwarz/Shutterstock.com**; p12, p30 (spider) © **D. Kucharski K. Kucharska/Shutterstock.com**; p13, 31 (mole) © **Marcin Pawinski/Shutterstock.com**; p14, 31 (fennec fox) © **hagit berkovich/Shutterstock.com**; p15 (elephant) © **Patryk Kosmider/Shutterstock.com**; p16, 31 (cuttlefish) © **Vilainecrevette/Shutterstock.com**; p17 (moth) © **Patrick Honan, Museum Victoria**; p18 (flamingo) © **zhaoyan/Shutterstock.com**; p19 (platypus), p30 (elephant seal) © **worldswildlifewonders/Shutterstock.com**; p19 (turtle) © **Rich Carey/Shutterstock.com**; p20, 31 (dragonfish) © **Julian Finn, Museum Victoria**; p21 (walrus) © **Vladimir Melnik/Shutterstock.com**; p22 (mosquito) © **Henrik Larsson/Shutterstock.com**; p23 (cicada) © **Steve Heap/Shutterstock.com**; p24 (rhinoceros hornbill) © **tratong/Shutterstock.com**; p26 (chameleon) © **fivespots/Shutterstock.com**; p27 (tiger) © **Arangan Ananth/Shutterstock.com**; p29 (stonefish) © **Ethan Daniels/Shutterstock.com**; p30 (damselfly) © **jmillerphoto /Shutterstock.com**; p31 (rhinoceros hornbill) © **apiguide/Shutterstock.com**; p32 (ostrich) © **ksyproduktor/Shutterstock.com**.

Funny
Faces

Dr Mark Norman

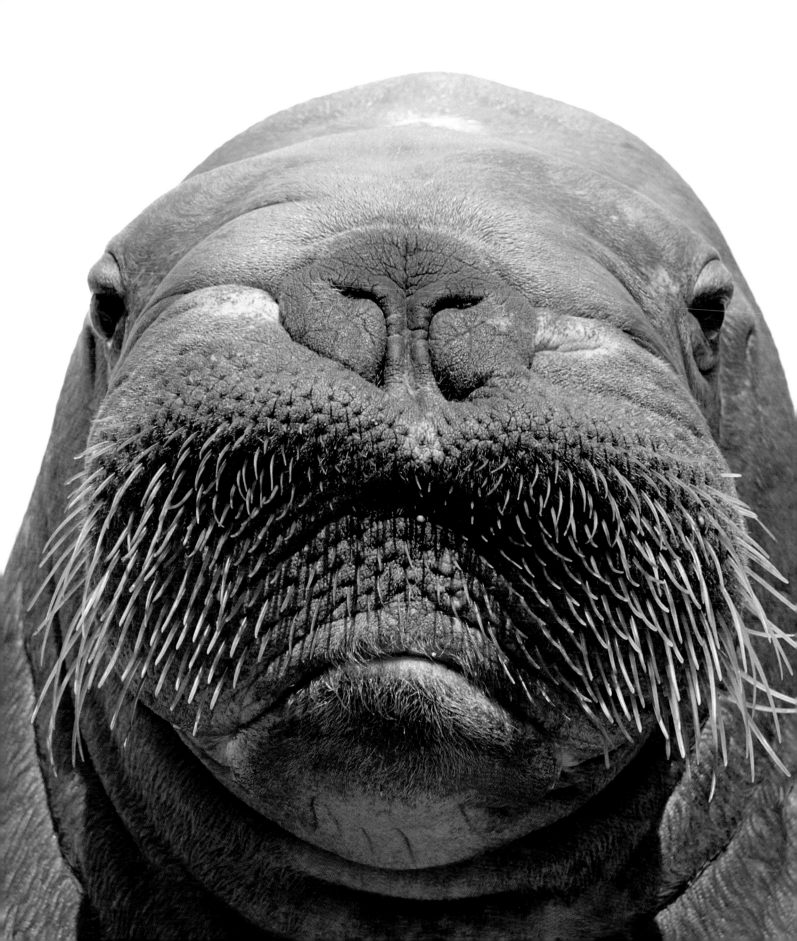

Different faces

The faces of some animals may look funny to us, but their eyes, ears, noses and mouths are exactly what those animals need to survive.

Big nose

Elephants are very heavy … and tall. Instead of bending awkwardly to the ground to drink and eat, they have long noses or trunks they use to gather water and food.

Male elephant seals have big floppy noses. They blow their hollow noses like loud trumpets to scare off other males.

Funny nose

The nose of a dolphin is on top of its head and it only has one nostril! It is called a blowhole and is used to breathe when swimming at the water's surface. If our nose was on top of our head, the rain would get in!

Bats that hunt insects often have a nose shaped like a flower. The nose sends out little squeaks that reach flying insects and bounce back to the bat's big ears. This works just like a ship's sonar and is how bats find their food in the dark.

Giant eyes

Tarsiers have large eyes for hunting spiders and grasshoppers at night. The bigger your eyes, the more light is let in so you can see better in the dark.

Dragonflies and damselflies have huge ball-like eyes that let them see in all directions when they're flying at high speed.

Funny eyes

A jumping spider has eight eyes! Six on the front and one on each side of its head. It uses all these eyes to search for food and also keep watch for any hungry birds that might try to eat them.

Moles live in tunnels underground where it is so dark that eyes are useless. Some species are blind, only having tiny eyes covered with skin. Instead, they use their noses and whiskers to feel for wriggling worms and bugs.

Big ears

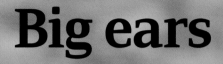

The fennec fox hunts at night in the desert. It uses its huge ears to hear the tiny scratching sounds of insects moving around on the sand.

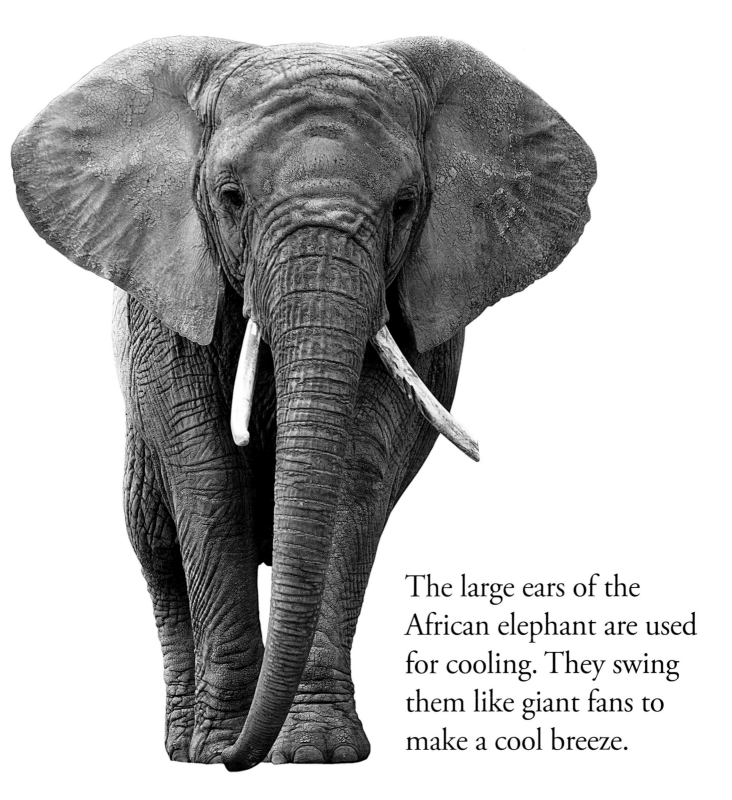

The large ears of the
African elephant are used
for cooling. They swing
them like giant fans to
make a cool breeze.

Arms on your face!

Cuttlefish have ten tentacles around their mouth. Each tentacle has lots of small gripping suckers to grab fish and crabs. Imagine if your arms and legs came off your lips!

Male moths have big feather-like antennae they use to smell the perfumes given off by female moths. If you look at moths flying around lights at night, you can tell which moths are male.

Strange beaks and bills

The flamingo has a beak made for using upside down! The flamingo bends its head down to the water and sweeps its beak from side to side to scoop up tiny shrimp.

18

A platypus has a bill like a duck. Both animals use their bills to dabble in the mud for small insects and shrimp.

Turtles have no teeth at all. Instead they have a sharp beak used for chopping up their food. Some turtles eat seagrass, while others eat jellyfish or sponges.

Teeth as tools

Walruses use their two long teeth like icepicks to pull themselves up out of the water onto floating sea ice.

Dragonfish live in the dark, deep sea where food is scarce so it can be a long time between meals. When they do catch something to eat they make 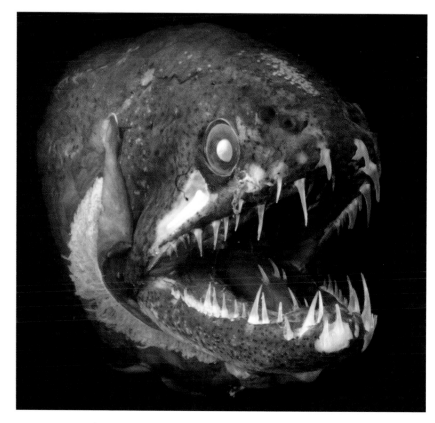 sure they hold on to it. That's why they have so many teeth – even some on their tongue!

Needle mouth

The sharp, pointed mouth of a female mosquito is made for jabbing into the skin and sucking up blood. A mosquito's saliva contains a painkiller so you don't feel anything until they pull the needle out.

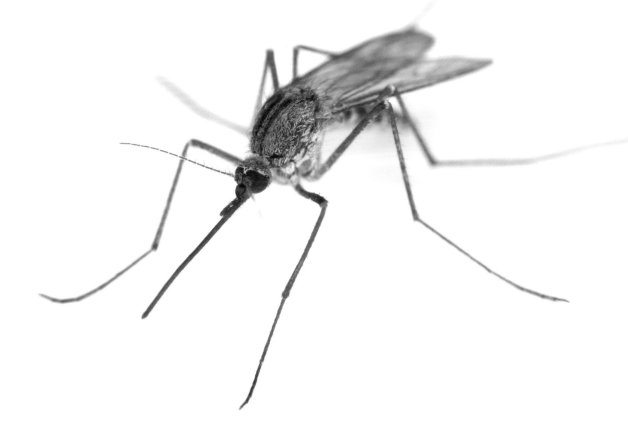

Cicadas use long thin mouthparts to drill into plants so they can drink the sap. They're like vampires that feed on the blood of trees.

Big hairdos

Many birds have a crest of feathers on the top of their heads that they use to signal to each other. When a cockatoo sees a predator coming, it lifts its crest and screeches an alarm.

The rhinoceros hornbill bird gets its name from the curved bump on top of its beak. The bump is hollow and makes the bird's call more musical.

Painted faces

The patterns on some animals' faces match where they live. The light and dark stripes on a tiger's face hide it amongst the leaves and shadows of the forest.

Chameleons are great at blending into their surroundings. Some even have leaf-like structures on the top of their heads that make them look like part of a plant. They stay perfectly still then shoot out their long sticky tongues to catch passing insects.

Hidden faces

In its natural environment a stick insect looks like a leaf or stick. This way birds can't see them. It's hard to even see their face.

A stonefish has a face that looks like a big piece of dead coral. It's invisible to passing fish. When they swim too close, the stonefish leaps up so fast that the fish never see it coming.

Fact files

Southern Elephant Seal *(Mirounga leonina)*

This animal gets its name from the short, fat trunk of the male seal. Males get very big, reaching six metres long and four tonnes! They live in Antarctica and nearby islands.

Persian Trident Bat *(Triaenops persicus)*

This bat is found in the Middle East and across East Africa. It hunts moths at night and roosts in huge numbers in caves during the day.

Philippine Tarsier *(Carlito syrichta)*

These tiny animals are not actually monkeys, but closely related to monkeys and humans. Their calls are so high-pitched that humans can't hear them. They live in the rainforests of the Philippine islands where logging threatens their homes.

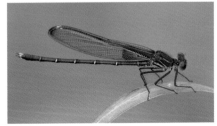

Damselfly (suborder *Zygoptera)*

Damselflies differ from dragonflies – a damselfly's wings lie along its body when resting, rather than flat and out to the side. Damselflies catch flies and mosquitoes while flying.

Jumping Spider (family *Salticidae)*

There are about 5000 species of jumping spiders found all over the world, from rainforests and deserts, to the slopes of Mount Everest. They mainly jump when hunting or escaping.

Blind Mole (*Talpa caeca*)

The blind mole is found in Europe where it lives underground beneath forests and meadows. It burrows through the deep soils, hunting for earthworms.

Fennec Fox (*Vulpes zerda*)

This tiny fox lives in the Sahara Desert in North Africa. It survives because it gets all the water it needs from the animals it eats. Its large ears can even hear insects moving underground.

Broadclub Cuttlefish (*Sepia latimanus*)

Cuttlefish are close relatives of octopus and squid. They can change the colour and texture of their skin to look like coral or seaweed. This way they are invisible to passing creatures.

Threadfin Dragonfish (*Echiostoma barbatum*)

This fish looks scary but is smaller than a banana! It lives at the bottom of the sea, down to four kilometres deep. It makes its own light as little spots along its body, on its cheeks and the tip of its chin.

Rhinoceros Hornbill (*Buceros rhinoceros*)

This big bird lives in Asian rainforests. It nests in tree hollows, where the male bird closes the entrance to the nest with mud, except for a small hole it uses to pass food to the female bird and the chicks.

Stick Insect (family *Phylliidae*)

Only male stick insects can fly. In some species, the babies impersonate (or look like) dangerous ants so they can walk around, searching for a good tree, without being eaten by birds or lizards.

Glossary

antennae: pair of feelers on the head of an insect or crustacean

coral: found in tropical waters, a hard red, pink or white substance that is formed by tiny sea creatures massed together

crest: a tuft of hair, skin, or feathers on an animal's head

dabble: splash something about in water

shrimp: a small shellfish

sonar: a device for finding objects under water by using bouncing soundwaves

tentacle: long, flexible part of an animal used to touch or hold

Index